THE RIMINI-FERRARA LINE

brendan connell

ISBN: 978-1-908125-63-7

Copyright 2018

Brendan Connell.

Cover design: David Rix

Interior design: Brendan Connell and David Rix

THE RIMINI-FERRARA LINE

YOU disks of steel with your yellow flashes—you stroboscopic tendril flying by in the night—or in the day waved at by children, dreaming of the ends of your far reaching arms, which stretch along the Adriatic, where the sturgeon play and the Pelagic pipefish compose their fantasias.

Out of the womb of Rimini you crawl, you great and glorious worm, out of that place where the Etruscans once dwelled and which fell like a head rolling to the Ostrogoths whose descendents now come to dip their feet in the water and piss away their bitter beer.

"Achtung!"

"Attenzione passeggeri . . ."

"Biglietti. Biglietti. Biglietti."

Squeak. Roll. Go!

Marco de Rippe stood next to the WC. It made him feel comfortable to stand there. He was 45 years old and wore glasses and looked unhappy. But he wasn't, though his father was hysteropathic and his mother a deaf mute. Fulzio Zamuto searched for old gum under his seat. There wasn't any and he was disappointed and felt like having a violent altercation. Delfo Nadalini believed himself to be a porcupine. In the driver's cabin Niccolò Arpino thought about bread. It was hard to get good bread. Real bread. Something so simple it was an insult something like an insult to be deprived of good things from times past so difficult to find. Silvia Boi stared. At nothing or was it eternity and then as they went she opened up her purse and took out a paperback copy of a book.

We echo friction—instant axle carrozza carrozza synchronous swerve we have frogs in our brain frogs the march march march march march along the labyrinthine way.

"Hello."

"Hello."

"You are reading."

"Yes."

"For work?"

"No."

"I am a designer of eyeglass frames. I did the F855. And your profession?"

"I have no employment."

"A difficult time this."

"Yes."

"Hard to make ends meet."

"Yes."

"Where are you getting off?"

"Ravenna."

"I could get off there too."

"Could you?"

"I could. If you wanted to make 100 euros. I could."

"???"

"There is an hotel by the station. Shabby enough. But what do we care? You. I. Together. Being alone together is the important thing. There are worse ways to make some change. I am going all the way to Ferrara, but I could be late. Very late."

Silvia closed her book.

"Excuse me," she said, "but aren't you the Prophet Elias?"

Climbing climbing up the ladder smart shock always climbing them hopping about in the brain you amphibians hopping about for intercommunication pulling at my tendons spiralling eel.

"Bellaria."

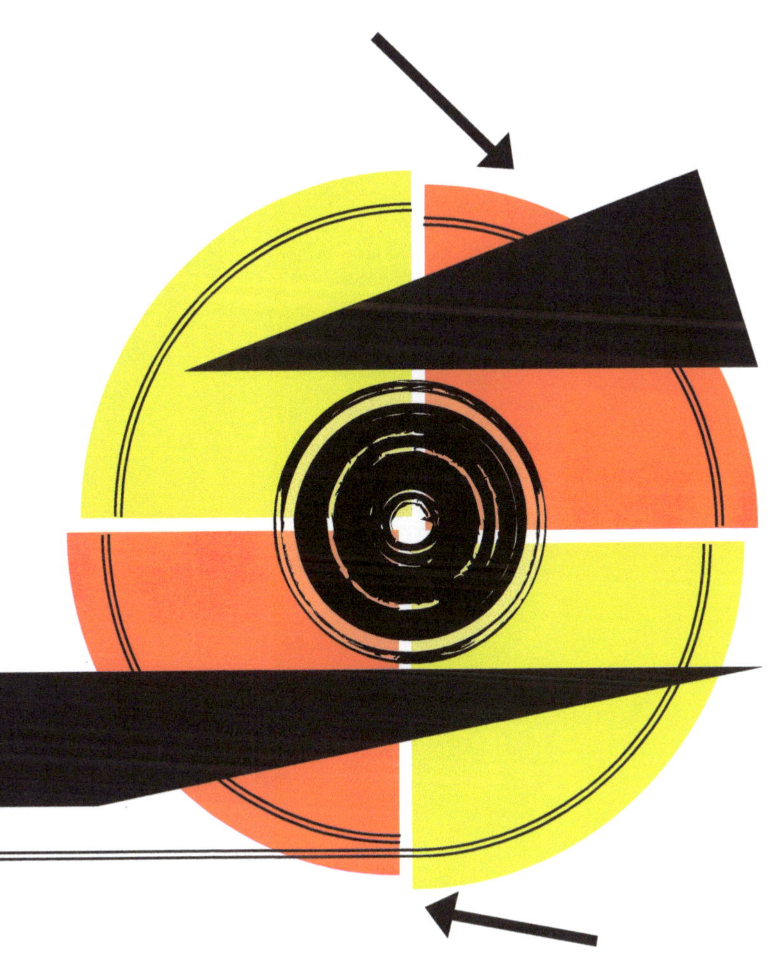

ORTIFIED farmyard steaming ra-
vine of nets breathed in by a green
bathing season.

Antonio Tosti, aged 27, got on and stood in the gangway, not far from Marco de Rippe, whose nostrils were dilated.

Go, you suns of steel; move that mighty pelvis.

Antonio had chestnut-coloured hair and eyes to match. He had entered a cloister at the age of 22, but after two years of such a life, his pulse became very slow. He was sent home and lay on his bed with his eyes closed, and when spoken to would only reply that he had been forbidden to com-municate. Fortunately, Dr. Adinolfi's private clinic in Bellaria had all the answers.

"This is the train for Berlin?" Antonio asked.

Marco's eyes opened wide.

At Gatteo a Mare a man by the name of Ettore Fanti got on. The night before he had stabbed his boyfriend in the thigh with a fork and afterwards had, after wiping the item of tableware clean, continued to eat his risotto alla pescatora.

Delfo Nadalini saw him approaching and bristled his quills. Ettore saw this and decided to sit a few seats back.

"Classe."

KKRIIK!

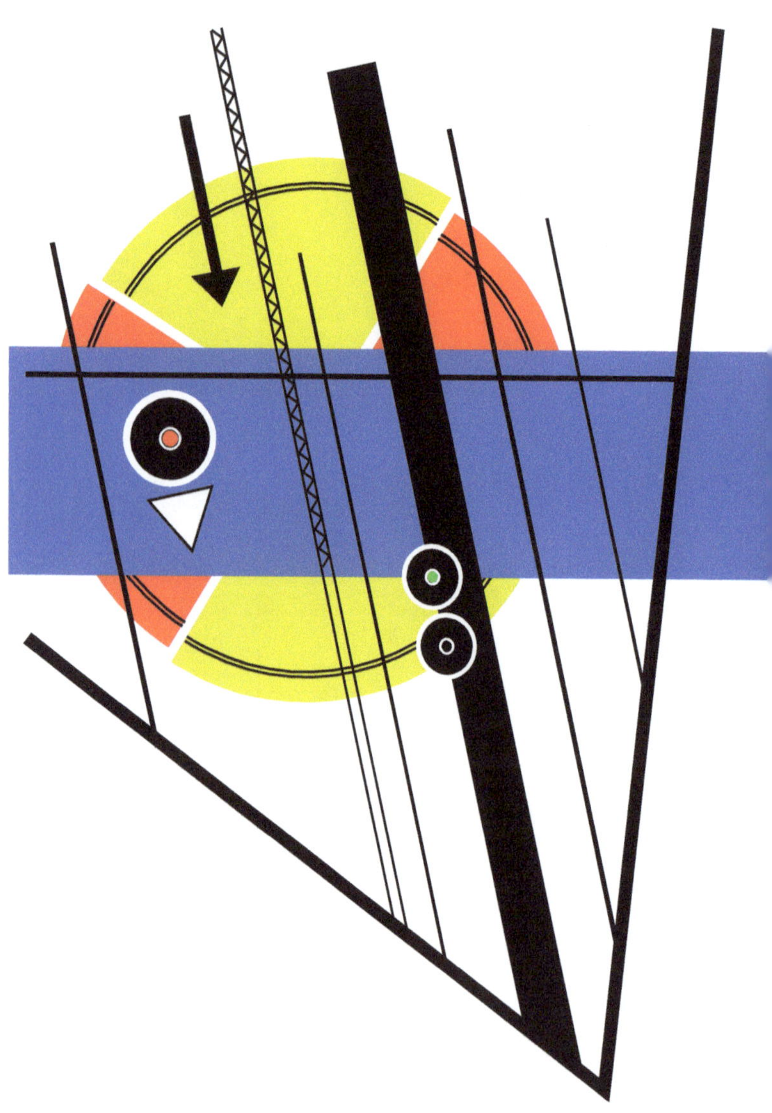

A LITTLE station. Get off if you want to see Sant'Apollinare/ ivory sheep on emerald grass. "Ravenna."

MARCO DE RIPPE looked at the WC longingly and then, when the doors opened, got off the train; in search of ice-cream.

The brick walls of the station drooled sweat. Off/on/mosaic of pickpockets and perverts bandaged up in tight jeans, of broke businessmen and bored mothers, of men who in ages past might have been emperors, but now scraped the shit from their shoes and counted the change in their pockets. Off/on.

An English couple leaped aboard, just as the train was about to depart.

"Venice? Venice? Venice?"

Silence.

The man walked pigeon-toed; the woman with a slight limp.

They thrust their buttocks on the saddles as the train sucked at its energy and leapt forward like a doe.

"Biglietti. Biglietti."

"Venice?"

"You go Venezia?"

"Yes. Venezia! Venezia!"

"You get off Ferrara. Change Venezia line."

"Ferrara?"

"Ferrrr-aaaa-raaa!"

Delfo Nadalini took out a cabbage sandwich and ate it.

Go you alligator, away from that prison of Thusnelda, go you navigant hound, and snake along through the mild weather the sun radiating your carriages.

Dizziness.

AT ALFONSINE it was the marriage season. Luca and Dora pulled their luggage on the train and sat down together. They anticipated the carnal connection of wedlock, though Luca (aged 26) was unaware that Dora (aged 22) considered herself to be the Queen of Heaven and hoped to give birth to the Saviour.

She smiled.

Yes, and if Luca caused her any problems, she'd whip the devil right out of him with a glad hand.

"Lavezzola."

"Excuse me, is this Ferrara?"

"Lavezzola."

"Pardon?"

"Lavezzola!"

K

C

C

K

S

NICCOLÒ ARPINO stared at the gauges and wondered what would be for dinner. He hoped his wife had made a torta for dessert. Not too sweet with these vegetative disturbances.

A Guardia di Finanza balanced on his heels.

FFFFH!

S IX TEENAGERS boarded the train:

1. Was turbulent.
2. Would kill himself at the age of 29; method: pesticide ingestion.
3. Would do nothing.
4. Had a tendency to tear her clothes.
5. Would do nothing.
6. Was turbulent, restless at night and full of desire during the day.

A CHINESE MAN by the name of Pi Shiying got on. He had just shot up a generous dosage of heroin in the toilette and was feeling good. He sat down and smiled.

"Biglietti. Biglietti. Biglietti."

Alvaro Pedrina, the ticket taker, was a poet. He composed the following lines:

> Maria, you are a frisky cat
> And every time I see you
> I wish you'd scratch my mouse

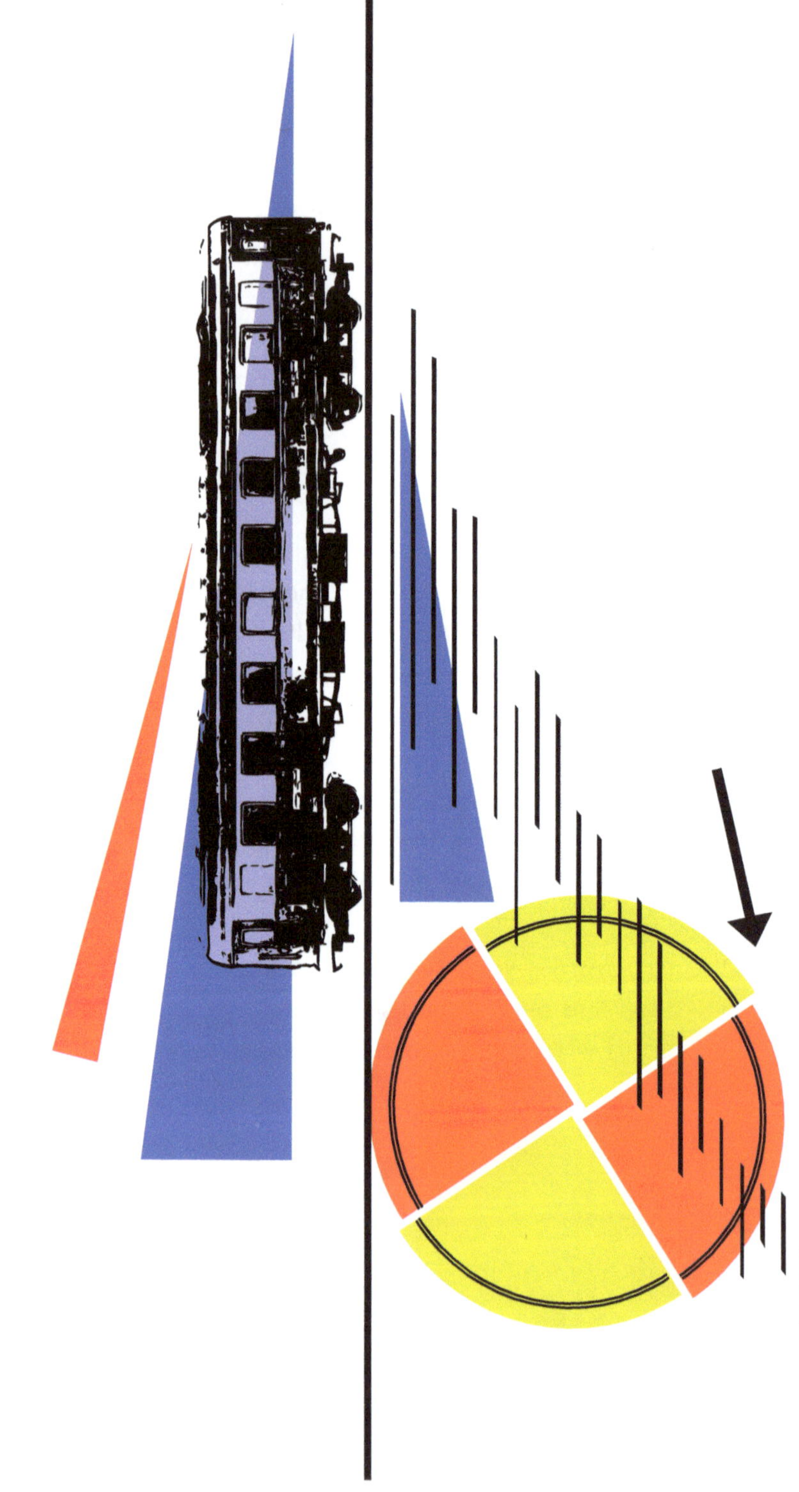

THE CARS sailed over the tracks.

Pi Shiying scratched his arm. Every night he dreamed that someone cut off his head and every morning awoke with his head on his shoulders.

"Portomaggiore."

A CONTINUATION of friction grinding with the carrozza carrozza onward on the march but who has superior wisdom with frogs in the brain wiggle couplings if we could run over the frog.

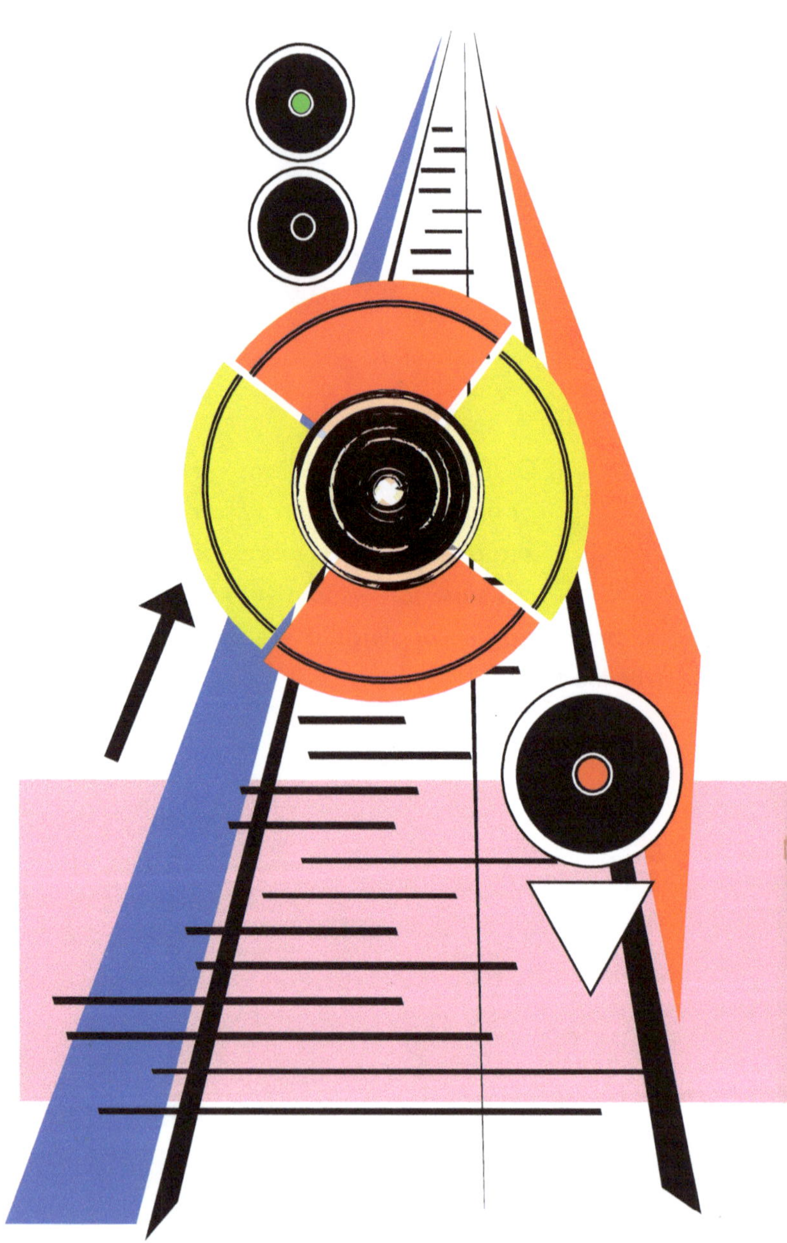

AT GAIBANELLA a man got on.

"Biglietti."

He reached in his pocket, took out a pebble and handed it to Alvaro.

"Ticket?'

"That's it!"

"It's a pebble."

"I assure you that it is a ticket!"

"Cazzo."

The end is never retard me never the end.

Everyone rose from their seats and made their way to the doors.

"Is this were we get off for Venice?"

"This is Berlin?"

"Berlin?"

"Venice?"

"Ferrara."

ISSN:

THE FINISHING LINE. Theft. Murder. Molestation. Drugs. Attempted murder. Rape. Pickpocket. Beatings—yes you great snake of steel, serpent of dreams, you red-eyed mare that harbours larceny of all descriptions, some macrocosmic sodomy with a cry of brakes—or is it trafficking in slaves you do? But no, you royal demon, sinuous dragon who tears through avidity and speculation, you hysterical machine vomiting your human cargo—it is you who the mobility worship and whose praises are sung.

www.ingramcontent.com/pod-product-compliance
Lightning Source LLC
Chambersburg PA
CBHW051526200726
48295CB00029B/939